8,000 STONES
A Chinese Folktale

8,000 STONES

A Chinese Folktale

Told by Diane Wolkstein

Illustrated by Ed Young

Doubleday & Company, Inc., Garden City, New York

Library of Congress Catalog Card Number 71-99466
Text Copyright © 1972 by Diane Wolkstein
Illustrations Copyright © 1972 by Ed Young
All Rights Reserved
Printed in the United States of America
First Edition

Long ago in China, there lived a very powerful ruler. He was known as the Most Supreme Govenor of China. His name was Ts'ao Ts'ao.

Ts'ao Ts'ao ruled the royal city of
Loyang and lived in a beautiful palace
surrounded by lovely gardens. The

treasures of the royal city and palace were well protected by the Governor's mighty army of 10,000 soldiers. But the neighboring kings and princes heard of Ts'ao Ts'ao's beautiful palace and mighty army, and they came themselves or sent messengers to see the wonders of the royal city.

The messengers often brought splendid
presents.
This year the Satrap, or prince, of
India sent Ts'ao Ts'ao a most unusual
present: a present that neither Ts'ao
Ts'ao nor anyone in Ts'ao Ts'ao's king-

dom had ever seen before. When the
Indian messengers arrived in Loyang,
the peasants came running from their
fields to see the marvelous creature.
The courtiers came out of the palace,
and soon a huge noisy crowd formed
around the animal.

Then Ts'ao Ts'ao appeared, and the Indian messengers, the peasants, and all the court knelt before him. "Rise!" Ts'ao Ts'ao commanded the Indian messengers. "Rise and explain the cause of this uproar. What is this beast doing in my kingdom?"

"It is a present," explained the messengers. "It is a present from the Grand Satrap of India to the Most Supreme Governor of China, Ruler of Loyang, General of 10,000 soldiers — Yourself!"

"Oh...oh yes," muttered Ts'ao Ts'ao. (He just then remembered that this was the time of year the Satrap's presents usually did arrive.)

"Delighted!" exclaimed Ts'ao Ts'ao. "The Grand Satrap of India is to be informed that I am delighted with his …his…what is it called, his…?"

"Elephant!" answered the messengers. Junma, the son of one of the Indian messengers, showed his small ivory elephant to P'ei, the son of Ts'ao Ts'ao. P'ei showed Junma his new Chinese sailboat.

"And how tall is my elephant?" asked Ts'ao Ts'ao.

"Ten feet tall, Most Supreme Governor of China."

"And how much does my elephant weigh?"

"Oh, we cannot tell you Most Supreme Governor. There are no scales in India large enough to weigh such an animal."

"You mean to say that the Grand Satrap of India does not know how much an elephant weighs?"

"That is correct, Most Supreme Governor of China."

"I see," said Ts'ao Ts'ao, "I see...."
When the Indian messengers had been
led into the palace to eat and rest,
Ts'ao Ts'ao called his advisers together:
"I want to know, before the messengers
leave at the end of the month, the exact

14

weight of my elephant. If the Grand Satrap of India does not know how to weigh an elephant, then I, Ts'ao Ts'ao, Ruler of Loyang, General of 10,000 soldiers shall show him the way!"

The advisers then spent all their time thinking:
How to weigh an elephant...?
How to weigh the Most Supreme Governor of China's elephant?
How to weigh the elephant?

But they could not think of a way. Then a week before the messengers were to leave, little P'ei came from playing with his sailboat to see the wonderful elephant.
"What are you doing under the

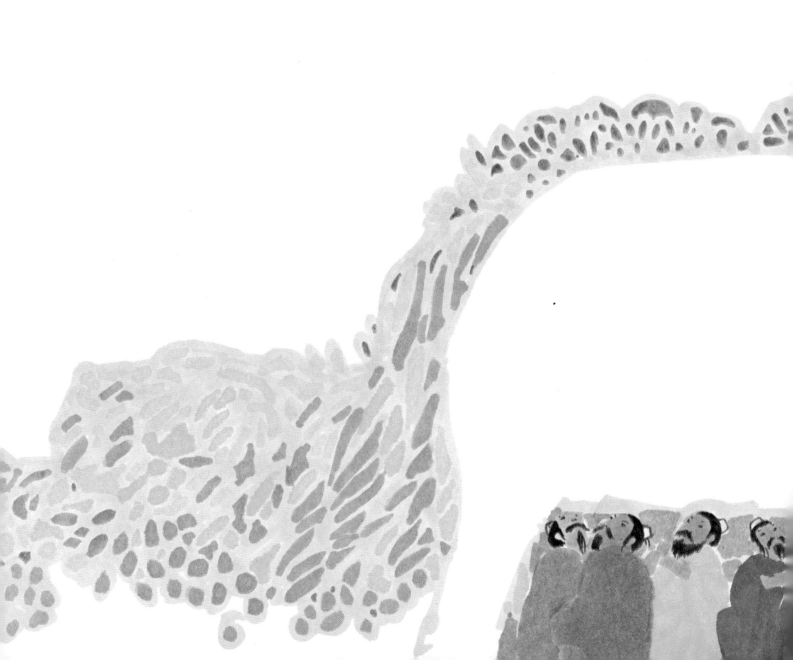

elephant?" he called to the advisers.
"Shhh...we're thinking."
"What about?" whispered P'ei.
"How to weigh an elephant," the
advisers whispered back.
"Well, that's not so hard," said P'ei.
"Not so hard?" cried the advisers.
"No," said P'ei. "Follow me, and I'll
show you."

19

P'ei led them through the woods to a small pond near the palace. There by the pond was P'ei's new toy sailboat.
It looked like any toy Chinese sailboat, except it had a strange line carved into its side.
"Wait here!" cried P'ei and he ran back to the palace.
The advisers picked up the boat. They examined the line carefully. At the side of the line was the Chinese character for elephant.
What did it mean?
The advisers shook their heads. They did not understand.
Little P'ei returned from the palace, carrying Junma's ivory elephant.
"Watch," he said to the advisers.
He placed the elephant on the sailboat and the boat sank in the water to the carved line.

"You see," P'ei explained, "no matter how many times I sailed Junma's elephant on my boat, it always weighed the boat down to that line, so I carved his character next to it. If you want to weigh the big elephant, you can do the same thing. And if you need to know the exact weight of the elephant, then pile stones on the boat until the boat sinks to the elephant's character."
"That's it! That's it!" cried the advisers. "Little P'ei, you've shown us the way."
On the day of the weighing, a large crowd of courtiers and peasants gathered around the shore of the palace lake.
The elephant was led from the fields onto a sturdy barge. Little P'ei and the advisers then stepped into a smaller boat.

Little P'ei was given the honor of carving, just above the water line, the character of the Most Supreme Governor of China's elephant on the barge.

After both boats were brought back to shore, the barge was pushed out again. Many stones were piled on it. It took many, many stones for the barge to sink to the character of the elephant. Can you guess how much the elephant weighed?

The elephant weighed 8000 stones. A gong was sounded and the announcement made by the court herald:

"The Most Supreme Governor of China's elephant weighs the Most High Amount of 8000 stones!"

The peasants cheered and the courtiers applauded.

The gong rang out again. This time Ts'ao Ts'ao, Most Supreme Governor of China, Ruler of Loyang, General of 10,000 soldiers spoke:

"Let it be known that the plan for the weighing of the Most Supreme Governor of China's elephant was thought of by none other than my own son...little P'ei."

The peasants, the advisers, and the courtiers cheered even louder.

"AND let it be written in the court annals, continued Ts'ao Ts'ao, "and a copy be given to the Indian messengers to present to the Grand Satrap of India."

So the story of little P'ei and the weight of the elephant were written out and presented to the Indian messengers to take back to the Satrap. And Ts'ao Ts'ao, Most Supreme Governor of China, then became famous—not only for his beautiful

palace and mighty army—but also for the Most Supreme Intelligence of his clever son...little P'ei.

In later years, little P'ei became Ts'ao P'ei, EMPEROR OF ALL OF CHINA. That was in a.d. 200, almost 2000 years ago.

About the Author

DIANE WOLKSTEIN, noted storyteller, is a Recreation Specialist for New York City's Park and Cultural Affairs Department. She tours parks, playgrounds, schools and libraries across the country telling children's stories. She also has a weekly radio program, STORIES FROM MANY LANDS.

About the Illustrator

ED YOUNG, a native of Shanghai, China, attended the University of Illinois, Art Center College of Design, and Pratt Institute. He has illustrated numerous successful books for children. He is at present teaching visual communication at Pratt Institute.

J

PZ 8.1 .W84 Ei 1972

Wolkstein, Diane

8,000 stones   lktale. Told
                                   y Ed Young.
                                  ., Doubleday
     [1972]
     27 p. col. illus. 20 x 24 cm.
   Retells the Chinese tale in which the
governor's clever son finds a way to weigh
an elephant.

     I. Young, Ed, illus. II. Title.